JUST ONE TOOTH

Also by Miriam Nerlove

I Made A Mistake
I Meant to Clean My Room Today

JUST ONE TOOTH

Miriam Nerlove

Margaret K. McElderry Books
NEW YORK

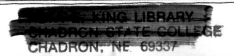

Margaret K. McElderry Books
Macmillan Publishing Company
866 Third Avenue
New York, NY 10022
Collier Macmillan Canada, Inc.

Text composition by Linoprint Composition, New York, New York.
Printed in Singapore

First Edition
10 9 8 7 6 5 4 3 2 1

Library of Congress Cataloging-in-Publication Data
Nerlove, Miriam.
Just one tooth.
Summary: When a little bear named Ruth loses her
beloved tooth, she doesn't believe the tooth fairy,
who says that a new tooth will grow in its place.
[1. Teeth—Fiction.   2. Bears—Fiction.
3. Stories in rhyme]   I. Title.
PZ8.3.N365Ju   1989   [E]   88-19488
ISBN 0-689-50465-9

For Eleanor, Susan, and Joe, with love

There was a little bear named Ruth,
Who had just one big, shiny tooth.

After meals and in between,
Ruth would brush her big tooth clean.

She brushed so hard to make it white,
The tooth shone like a star at night.

But one day while Ruth drank her juice,
Ruth could feel her tooth come loose.

The tooth then popped onto the floor
And rolled beneath the kitchen door.

Ruth cried at first and was quite sad—
She'd lost the only tooth she had.

Her mother tried to comfort her
And dried the tears that soaked Ruth's fur.

A fairy came that night to Ruth
And promised her another tooth.

Ruth checked the mirror every day
Before she went outside to play.

She even tried to brush the space
Where once her tooth had been in place.

A whole month passed and still no tooth—
The fairy hadn't told the truth!

And then one day Ruth felt a bump
That turned into a small white lump.

Slowly there emerged a tooth,
Shining brightly, just for Ruth.

Ruth brushed her tooth and showed her mother
That sure enough—she'd grown another!